# By the light of the MOON

## TOM PERCIVAL

BEST
TOYS

VaN'S
TuFF

BLOOMSBURY
LONDON OXFORD NEW YORK NEW DELHI SYDNEY

Moving house is a
BIG thing for most people.
And so it was for Ivan . . .

Ivan's old house had always been so **warm** and **friendly**.

*This* new one was NOT.

It was all so . . .

*strange*.

And his new bedroom felt strangest of all.

He stared up at the moon,
just as he *used* to in
the old house.

And *that* was
when something
unusual happened . . .

A shimmering light drifted down to land
in the garden. Ivan's heart fluttered.

*What could it be?*

He dashed through
the house . . .

and out into the night.

*There* was the ball of light!
Ivan ran towards it . . .

. . . but the light skipped **away**,

leading him from
rock to stream,

and flower to tree,

until all of a sudden, it vanished.

There was a flash of light
and a small, furry
*something* appeared.

It had stripes on its tail
and a friendly face.

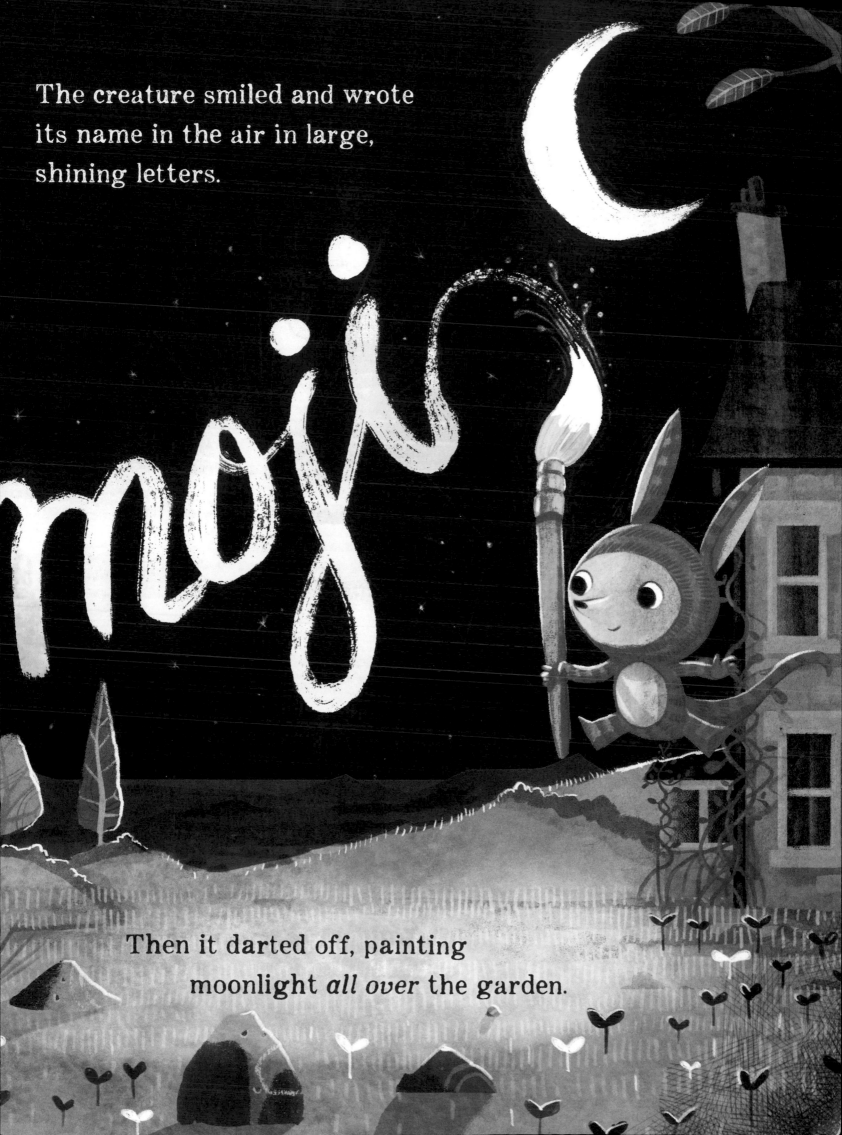

The creature smiled and wrote
its name in the air in large,
shining letters.

*moji*

Then it darted off, painting
moonlight *all over* the garden.

Ivan gasped as
the trees grew
ten times taller and
*everything* came to life.

Then the Moji painted Ivan with moonlight too.

He grew lighter,
and lighter,
**and *lighter*,**

until . . .

He was flying,
he was *really* flying!

Ivan laughed as they soared up.
Higher than the clouds . . .

higher than the stars . . .

. . . until he could *almost*
touch the moon!

Then they swept back down to earth.
Together they danced through deep forests,
leapt from island to island . . .

and even
explored
underwater.

Ivan had *never* felt so happy.

But all too soon the adventure was over.
The Moji turned to Ivan
and painted one word . . .

"But *this* is not my home,"
said Ivan. "Not *really*."

The Moji smiled
and lit up the sky
with pictures . . .

pictures of Ivan in
the new house.

*Happy* pictures.

And Ivan understood.
The new house might not
feel like home *yet* . . .

but one day soon
– *it would.*

The Moji nodded and painted one
last word into the sky.

Goodbye

NEW MOON  YOUNG  WAXING CRESCENT  WAXING QUARTER  WAXING GIBBOUS

FULL  WANING GIBBOUS  WANING QUARTER  WANING CRESCENT  OLD

NEW MOON  YOUNG  WAXING CRESCENT  WAXING QUARTER  WAXING GIBBOUS

FULL  WANING GIBBOUS  WANING QUARTER  WANING CRESCENT  OLD

The letters hung there
for a moment until they –
like the Moji – were gone.